SEAS AND OCEANS

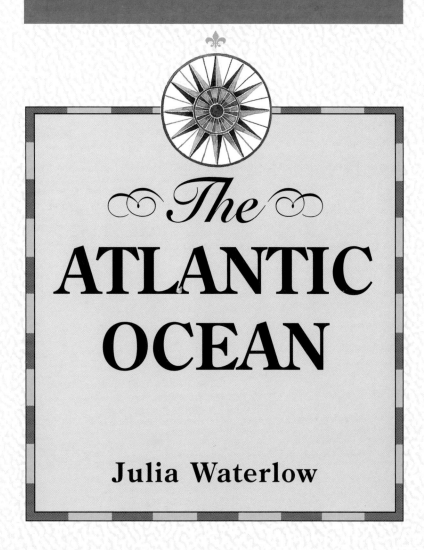

The ATLANTIC OCEAN

Julia Waterlow

RSVP

RAINTREE
STECK-VAUGHN
PUBLISHERS
The Steck-Vaughn Company

Austin, Texas

Seas and Oceans series

The Atlantic Ocean
The Caribbean and the Gulf of Mexico
The Indian Ocean
The Mediterranean Sea
The North Sea and the Baltic Sea
The Pacific Ocean
The Polar Seas
The Red Sea and the Arabian Gulf

Cover: Rough seas crash into the granite cliffs of south-west Cornwall.

© **Copyright 1997, text, Steck-Vaughn Company**

Published by Raintree Steck-Vaughn Publishers,
an imprint of Steck-Vaughn Company

Library of Congress Cataloging-in-Publication Data
Waterlow, Julia.
The Atlantic Ocean / Julia Waterlow.
    p.   cm.—(Seas and oceans)
Includes bibliographical references (p.   ) and index.
Summary: Presents information about the second-largest ocean including its plant life, fishing and mineral resources, use for transporting settlers and cargo, and problems with pollution.
ISBN 0-8172-4509-X
1. Oceanography—Atlantic Ocean—Juvenile literature.
[1. Atlantic Ocean. 2. Oceanography.]
I. Title. II. Series: Seas and oceans (Austin, Tex.)
GC481.W37   1997
551.46'1—dc20   96-8352

Printed in Italy. Bound in the United States.
1 2 3 4 5 6 7 8 9 0 01 00 99 98 97

Picture acknowledgments:

Finn G. Andersen 6; Dieter Betz 35 (top), 45; Ecoscene 4–5 (Andrew D. R. Brown), 9 (Julie Meech), 34 (Julie Meech), 38 (Nick Hawkes); Mary Evans 20; Eye Ubiquitous *cover, 32*; Geoscience Features 10–11, 12, 39; Frank Lane Picture Agency 14 (D. P. Wilson), 24 (E. and D. Hosking), 37, 44 (D. Coutts); Life File 41 (left/Nigel Sitwell), 42 (Nigel Sitwell); Impact 28 (bottom/Guy Moberly); Kaare Øster 25; Kattegatcentret, Grenaa 16 (bottom); Papilio 13, 17 (inset); Science Photo Library 36; Tony Stone 43 (Martin Rogers); Julia Waterlow 8, 18, 21, 27, 28–9, 30–31 (bottom); Zefa 15, 16–17 (top/Ziesler), 22, 26, 31 (top), 33 (Nakada), 41 (right).

All artwork is produced by Hardlines except Stephen Chabluk 35 (bottom).

Contents

Words that appear in **bold** in the text can be found in
the glossary on page 46.

INTRODUCTION
A Watery Giant

Facts and figures	
Area	31,650,000 sq. mi.
Average depth	11,800 ft.
Maximum depth	31,365 ft. (Puerto Rico Trench)
Volume	11,500,000 cu. ft.
Surface temperatures	77°F (at equator) 42°F (at 70 °N) 30°F (at 70 °S)

The Atlantic Ocean is named after Atlas, the mythical giant who carried the world on his shoulders. It is a huge expanse of water, the second-largest ocean in the world after the Pacific. Stretching from the Arctic in the north, it curves in a long S-shape across the **equator** to the Antarctic in the south.

The Atlantic can be divided into two parts, the North Atlantic and the South Atlantic, roughly divided by the equator. To the west lie the Americas and to the east, Europe and Africa. At Cape Horn, the southernmost tip of South America, the South Atlantic meets the Pacific; at the Cape of Good Hope in southern Africa, its waters merge into the Indian Ocean.

Although there are many islands, especially along the coasts of the North Atlantic, out in the middle of the ocean there are relatively few islands compared with the Pacific Ocean.

Even though its waters are vast, in the last few hundred years people have developed ways to cross the Atlantic safely and quickly. It became an important highway for trade after the Americas were discovered and settled by Europeans, and it is still one of the busiest seas in the world.

The Atlantic is important to the people who live on its shores. It not only affects the weather on land, but also has useful **natural resources**. Its waters are a source of fish for food, the seabed contains minerals, and people come to enjoy the long and beautiful coastlines and to see the ocean wildlife.

Even though the Atlantic is large, its waters and wildlife are being damaged by the way humans use it. Waste of all kinds is dumped into the sea, and fish are caught in huge numbers. Even though people have explored the surface waters, the great depths below remain among the least-known parts of our planet. We still have much to learn about how our use of the ocean will affect life in the Atlantic in the future.

Left: *The sea off the Cornish coast in Great Britain is one of the stormiest parts of the Atlantic. Here, waves and wind have eroded the shale cliffs, leaving a rugged coastline and rocky outcrops.*

Below: *The Atlantic Ocean separates the Americas from Europe and Africa in a wide S-shape. This map shows some of the main fringing seas, nations, islands, and rivers.*

Arctic Ocean

GREENLAND

ICELAND

North Sea

SCANDINAVIA

Baltic Sea

North Atlantic Ocean

NEWFOUNDLAND

CANADA

BRITAIN

IRELAND

Bay of Biscay

FRANCE

St Lawrence

USA

Cape Cod

AZORES

SPAIN

Mediterranean Sea

Cape Hatteras

MADEIRA

MOROCCO

Sargasso Sea

BERMUDA

CANARY IS.

Gulf of Mexico

MEXICO

CUBA

MAURITANIA

Caribbean Sea

CAPE VERDE ISLANDS

Niger

NIGERIA

LIBERIA

IVORY COAST

Congo

Equator

Amazon

Pacific Ocean

BRAZIL

ASCENSION IS.

ANGOLA

ST HELENA

NAMIBIA

SOUTH AFRICA

URUGUAY

South Atlantic Ocean

Cape of Good Hope

N

ARGENTINA

TRISTAN DA CUNHA

FALKLAND IS.

Cape Horn

0	miles	3000
0	km	5000

The Shape of the Atlantic

About 200 million years ago all the **continents** of the world were joined together in a great landmass, Pangaea, which was surrounded by a vast ocean, Panthalassa. Slowly, the landmass broke up, and the pieces spread to form continents. Looking at the shapes of South America and Africa today, we can get a good idea of how these lands were once joined. As these two continents moved apart, water filled the space, creating the Atlantic Ocean.

The continents lie on huge plates of solid rock. These plates float like rafts on a layer of molten rock beneath the earth's surface. Where the plates join, molten rock forces its way through, sometimes appearing violently in **volcanic** eruptions. The molten rock is so hot that volcanoes can even occur underwater.

Down the middle of the Atlantic two of these great plates are moving apart very slowly, at a rate of about one-half inch a year. Along this line molten rock has oozed out of the earth and cooled to form an underwater mountain range called the Mid-Atlantic Ridge. Although the molten rock usually flows gently, occasionally great eruptions bring rock above sea

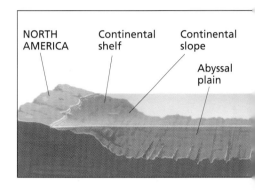

NORTH AMERICA · Continental shelf · Continental slope · Abyssal plain

Above: *The main feature of the Atlantic Ocean floor is a chain of undersea mountains called the Mid-Atlantic Ridge.*

Right: *The floor of the Atlantic Ocean is not smooth. There are mountains and trenches just as there are on land.*

Mid-Atlantic Ridge

Azores – the peaks of underwater volcanoes

West Africa has little or no continental shelf

AFRICA

Below: *The continents have moved around over millions of years. Oceans have been created and then destroyed.*

The Continents

Panthalassa   PANGAEA   Tethys   Panthalassa

175 million years ago

50 million years ago

Left: *Many Atlantic islands are the peaks of underwater volcanoes. This is Mount Teide on the island of Tenerife in the Canary Islands. It rises 12,200 feet out of the water. The volcano's last major eruption happened 300 years ago, and it still shows signs of life.*

St Lawrence

North Atlantic

EUROPE

North American Basin

MID-ATLANTIC RIDGE

AFRICA

Cape Verde Basin

Niger

Amazon

SOUTH AMERICA

Angola Basin

Congo

Plate

Cape Basin

Argentine Basin

South Atlantic

N

0   miles   2000

0   km   4000

level. Many of the islands of the Atlantic, from Iceland in the north to Tristan da Cunha in the south, are the peaks of undersea mountains formed in this way.

Around the edges of the continents the Atlantic is quite shallow, in most places less than 1,800 feet deep. Coastal waters cover a shelf of rock, known as the **continental shelf**, which continues out underwater about 45 miles from the shore. The continental shelf is much wider in the North Atlantic than in the South; off the west coast of Africa the continental shelf is extremely narrow. At the edge of the continental shelf, the seabed slopes down to about 13,000 feet, leveling out onto a great underwater plain, called the abyssal plain.

FEATURES OF THE OCEAN
Coasts

The long coastlines of the Atlantic have every kind of coastal feature, molded by wind, waves, and sea currents. The most rugged and rocky coasts are found in the far North and South Atlantic. Along many of the European coastlines, stormy Atlantic waves crash into high cliffs.

Over the last 10,000 years the level of the ocean has risen and many coastlines have been flooded. In some places, river valleys have filled with water, making deepwater **estuaries**, such as Chesapeake Bay and Falmouth in Great Britain. Here, large ships can enter and moor.

Sand is formed as waves break and grind rock into smaller and smaller pieces. There are thousands of miles of sandy beaches along Atlantic coastlines, especially where the land slopes gently to the ocean. Some of the longest stretches of beach in the world are along the Brazilian and West African coasts.

Below: In 1909, this ship ran aground in shallow coastal waters off Namibia, Africa. Over the years, the wind has gradually blown desert sand into the sea, and sea currents have swept sand along the coast, changing the shape of the shoreline. Now the ship lies in the desert several hundred yards inland from the Atlantic.

Above: Mangrove trees, such as these in Gambia, are common around river estuaries along tropical coastlines. Here, freshwater from the river meets saltwater from the sea, which covers the roots of the mangroves at high tide. Unlike other trees, mangroves have adapted to survive in salty ocean water.

Sea currents and waves sweep away small pieces of material like sand and then drop them elsewhere. Sometimes they pile sand and mud into long ridges called bars and spits, like those at Cape Hatteras, North Carolina. Much of the Atlantic coast of the United States from Cape Cod southward has an offshore line of sandbars and beaches. Behind lie **lagoons**, where the sheltered waters are often salty and marshy.

The Atlantic has more rivers draining into it than any other ocean. Rivers bring huge amounts of sand, **silt,** and clay down to the coast, and these materials are dropped in and around river mouths and even out at sea. Rivers like the Amazon and the Niger have made **deltas** several hundreds of miles wide, where there are channels of water between sandbanks and islands of mud. Plants like the **tropical** mangrove take root in these low-lying marshy areas where freshwater mingles with saltwater from the Atlantic.

Currents

Water in the oceans is always moving. Where it has a regular flow in one direction, like a river, it is called an ocean current. Winds push the warm, tropical waters of the Atlantic near the equator westward. When it reaches the Americas, this warm current turns north and south. In the far north and far south of the Atlantic, winds blow eastward, pushing water back to the eastern edges of the ocean. The result is two huge, circular current systems, or gyres, one turning clockwise in the North Atlantic and one turning counterclockwise in the South Atlantic.

In the North Atlantic, the current that flows north from the Equator is called the Gulf Stream. It sweeps up the U.S. coast at a rate of more than 80 miles a day, taking warm water far to the north and across the Atlantic as far as Great Britain. The Gulf Stream is important because it brings to the northern United States and Great Britain very mild winters compared with other areas that lie at similar **latitudes**. The warming effects of this current can be felt even in the Arctic, where the Russian port of Murmansk stays ice-free year-round.

Another Atlantic current with an important effect on climate is the Benguela Current in the South Atlantic, which pushes cold water northward from the Antarctic Ocean along the coast of southwest Africa. As well as cooling temperatures in what would otherwise be a hot, tropical climate, the cold current stops rain from falling over the land. Cold air cannot carry water for long, and when warm and wet onshore winds are cooled by the current, they are forced to drop their rain over the sea. By the time winds reach the coast, they are dry. The result is a band of desert, the Namib, running the length of the southwest African coast.

From Tropical Seas to Icebergs

From warm waters near the equator, the Atlantic gradually becomes cooler, until it finally meets the icy waters of the Arctic and Antarctic. In the far north, the cold Labrador Current sweeps down the Canadian coast from the Arctic and meets the Gulf Stream near Newfoundland. The difference in temperature causes heavy sea fogs, which can be dangerous to shipping. More dangerous still are icebergs that the cold current sometimes brings south. In this area in 1912, an iceberg sank the *Titanic*, the largest passenger ship at the time on its first voyage across the Atlantic. Hundreds of passengers and crew were drowned as the ship went down.

Right: Currents circulate in the Atlantic moving water like rivers in the sea. This map shows some of the main surface currents.

Below: Huge icebergs drift south, passing between the coasts of Greenland and Canada into the North Atlantic. Only the tip of the iceberg can be seen—most of it lies underwater.

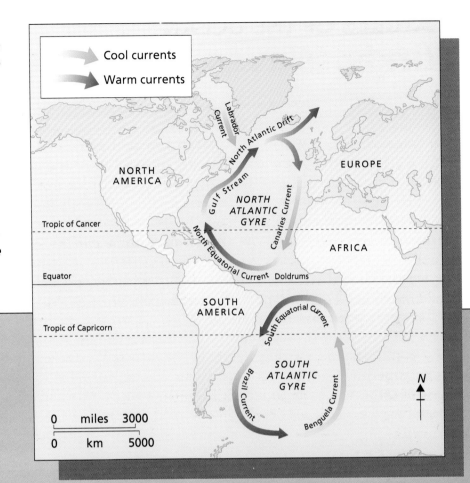

Winds, Waves, and Tides

Atlantic winds have always been important to sailors. The Trade Winds, which blow westward near the equator, made Christopher Columbus's voyage across the Atlantic possible. Columbus was able to return using the Westerlies, the winds that blow from west to east nearer to the poles. Lying on the equator itself is a band of calm water known as the Doldrums, where sailors can drift for days without wind.

The stormiest waters of the Atlantic lie in the far north and far south. In the North Atlantic, the Bay of Biscay is famous for its rough seas, and there are also storms off the rocky coasts of Great Britain, which have caused many shipwrecks. In the South Atlantic, swirling currents and strong Westerlies cause dangerous seas around Cape Horn. In tropical Atlantic seas, **hurricanes** sometimes build and sweep westward, devastating the southeast coast of the United States.

Below: Large oceans and seas have tides. In the Atlantic there are two tides a day. At low tide in this wide, shallow bay, the water uncovers huge expanses of sand.

Above: Waves and currents can gradually wear away coastlines, carrying sand and stones from one part of the coast and dumping them on another. To help slow erosion, concrete or wooden breakwaters are built along some beaches, like these on the south coast of Great Britain.

Waves are caused by the wind and can be anything between a ripple and 100 feet high. Although waves can sink ships, most of the damage caused by waves occurs on the coast where the waves break.

Twice a day the waters of the Atlantic rise and fall as tides. The height of tides is not the same all over the Atlantic and is usually greater on the continental shelves and in bays. One of the largest **tidal ranges** in the Atlantic is in the Bay of Fundy, Canada, where the tide can be as high as 42 feet. Atlantic tides can reach a long way up rivers as well—along the St. Lawrence River, Canada, the effect of the tide can be felt 930 miles away from the mouth of the river.

LIFE IN ATLANTIC WATERS
Plankton and the Food Chain

Life in the Atlantic varies from the tiniest creatures that can only be seen with a microscope to the largest animals on Earth, whales. Most important of all are the smallest forms of plant and animal life, known as plankton. These minute creatures and plants are eaten by fish and many other sea creatures. Smaller fish and other animals then become food for larger kinds of sea life. This arrangement is called a food chain, and plankton are the basic food on which other creatures depend.

Plant plankton need sunlight, so they float close to the surface. They also need nutrients: basic substances such as minerals that are dissolved in the water. Good supplies of nutrients are found in shallow, coastal areas where they are washed into the sea from the land and also where they are brought to the surface from the depths of the ocean by cold currents.

In the Atlantic, plankton grow particularly well in the very far north and far south, and off the west coast of Africa, because all of these areas are well supplied with nutrients from cold, deep waters. Because plankton provide food for so many sea creatures, these parts of the sea are also rich in other forms of ocean life. There is far less life out in the open Atlantic away from the shore.

Like plankton, most creatures live near the ocean surface. Many Atlantic fish swim in big schools, and some of the most common are anchovies, sardines, cod, halibut, and hake. There are also fast-swimming fish like sharks and swordfish that hunt smaller fish. Most seaweeds are usually found in water that is less than 160 feet deep because they need sunlight to grow.

Below: Seen with the help of a microscope, these tiny plankton are the basis of life in seas and oceans. Many sea creatures feed on them.

*Above: Whales are **mammals** and have to come to the surface to breathe air. Many live off plankton, but this beluga whale feeds mainly off small fish. It is found in cold Atlantic waters on the edge of the Arctic.*

Atlantic waters become colder and darker as they become deeper. No sunlight ever reaches the great depths of the Atlantic Ocean, so no plants can live down there. The few creatures that live on the bottom of the ocean rely on food in the form of dead plants and animals that sink from the upper ocean.

Feeding and Moving

Many creatures, from those as small as barnacles to those as large as whales, strain tiny pieces of food such as plankton out of the water in a process called filtering. Others, such as the sea anemone and the octopus, wait for their prey to come within reach and then trap it using tentacles. Many fish in the Atlantic chase their food. Sharks sometimes hunt together, surrounding schools of fish such as herring before moving in to kill, using razor-sharp teeth.

Sea creatures need some kind of defense to avoid the hunters. Crabs are protected by hard shells. Others camouflage themselves so they are difficult to spot. Mackerel have dark backs and shiny bellies, which makes it difficult to see them from either above or below. Squid manage to confuse their attackers by squirting a jet of dark ink, and then they dart away quickly.

Some fish, such as tuna, can swim at great speed and cover as much as 150 miles a day. Other creatures, such as mussels, attach themselves to rocks and never move. Some creatures, such as the large, jellyfish-like animal, the Portuguese man-of-war, just float and drift with winds and currents. Squid can swim using their fins, but when they have to move quickly, they can suck in and squirt out water like a jet.

Above: Flamingos feed in muddy waters on the shoreline, eating minute creatures that they strain through their beaks. Huge flocks of flamingos can be seen in some shallow bays on Atlantic shores in Africa.

Left: Sandbar sharks (top) and sandtiger sharks (bottom) are found along the Atlantic coast of the U.S. and the north of Africa. Sandbar sharks come in close to the shore to feed.

Above: *Crabs such as this shore crab live on the water's edge. They can survive in or out of the water and shelter in cracks in rocks or burrow in the sand. Their hard shells protect them from predators and from being knocked around by waves.*

Mammals that swim in the Atlantic all need to surface regularly to breathe. Whales can stay underwater for as long as an hour, diving as deep as 4,000 feet. Although whales and dolphins live in the water all the time, seals can be seen on many Atlantic coasts when they come ashore. Once out of water, the seals drag themselves along, but when they are in the ocean chasing fish, they are very good swimmers.

Most Atlantic birds fly, but many, like cormorants and puffins, can also swim underwater when they dive in to catch fish. Penguins are found on the islands and southern coasts of South America, and although they cannot fly or walk very well, they can swim like fish.

LIFE IN ATLANTIC WATERS
Migration

Right: This map shows the long journeys that eels make across the Atlantic Ocean to and from the Sargasso Sea.

Many sea creatures make regular journeys, called **migrations**, around the Atlantic, either every year or only once or twice in a lifetime. The main reasons for migrations are to find food or to breed. In the colder months, whales such as baleen whales head for warmer tropical waters, where they breed. They then migrate north and south as far as 1,800 miles to feed in the plankton-rich cold waters nearer the Arctic and Antarctic during the warmer weather.

Some fish migrate between freshwater and saltwater. Two or three times in their lives, North Atlantic salmon leave the ocean to travel up rivers far inland. Here they lay their eggs. When the small fish are large enough, they make the long journey back to the ocean. Amazingly, the salmon can recognize the rivers where they were born and return there when it is time to breed.

Turtles also migrate long distances, and they are found around many Atlantic coasts, especially in the warm, shallow waters off Brazil and the Atlantic coast of western Africa.

Right: A seal on the Atlantic coast of southwest Africa. Every year more than 100,000 seals come to breed at this particular place. When they are big enough, the young seal pups leave to hunt for fish on their own. Although they often swim far away, they return to the breeding area to have their own pups.

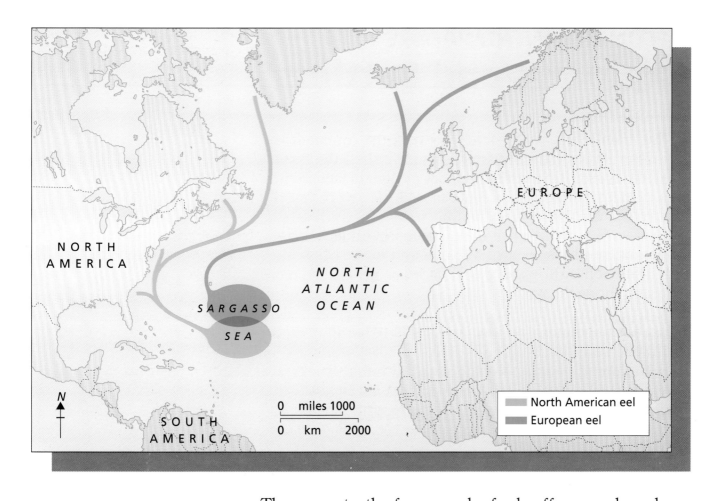

North American eel
European eel

Sargasso Sea

In the middle of the western Atlantic is a relatively calm area of water known as the Sargasso Sea. Floating on the surface are thick layers of seaweed, which provide food for all sorts of small sea creatures. In the Sargasso Sea, freshwater eels from North America and Europe come to spawn. The young eels, called elvers, are carried by the Gulf Stream toward the rivers where the adult eels came from. There they stay and feed until they are fully grown and then make the return journey back thousands of miles to the Sargasso Sea to breed.

The green turtle, for example, feeds off seaweeds and sea grasses in one coastal area, and then, every two or three years, the females leave to find a beach where they lay their eggs in the sand. The breeding areas can be hundreds of miles away from the feeding areas. Some green turtles are known to travel from Brazil as far as Ascension Island, 1,000 miles away. Like salmon, turtles return to the same place they hatched to breed.

Birds make the longest migrations of all. The small wading bird, the knot, migrates 10,000 miles every year from its breeding grounds in the far North Atlantic to the southern end of Africa and South America. Knots follow the coasts, stopping along the way for rest and food at the same places each time.

SETTLEMENT AND PEOPLE
Explorers and Settlers

The Atlantic is a huge barrier between the continents on either side. In ancient times people fished the waters along the coasts, but few ventured out of sight of land in their small boats. Neither the Americas or Africa were heavily populated, and the native people were mostly hunters, herders, or farmers who had no reason to leave their shores.

In Europe, **civilizations** developed in which people had more time and money to explore. The earliest Atlantic explorers were thought to be the Phoenicians, who were great traders in the Mediterranean region. About 450 B.C. a Phoenician expedition sailed south along the African coast searching for new lands and people to trade with. Although there are **legends** about earlier crossings, it was not until 1000 A.D. that Vikings made the first daring journey across the Atlantic and reached the Americas.

During the fifteenth century it was again Europeans who developed the skills and built the ships that made frequent journeys across such a huge stretch of water possible. The countries that faced the Atlantic, in particular Great Britain, France, Portugal, and Spain, were the first to explore and map the unknown ocean.

Above: An engraving showing Bartholomew Diaz in 1488 on his way to the Cape of Good Hope.

Their ships took them to many places along the Atlantic coasts of the Americas, where they built **trading posts** and then larger settlements. The explorers claimed the lands they found for their countries and fought wars with the native people, and each other, to obtain more territory. Along African coasts, Europeans set up ports for trading in ivory, gold, and **slaves**. Nearly every country facing onto the Atlantic became a **colony** of one European country or another.

These early explorers and the countries they came from still have a great influence on the people who live around the Atlantic today. As well as language (for example, Brazilians speak Portuguese, the rest of South America uses Spanish, Americans speak English and some Canadians use French), many countries keep the religions and culture of the European country that once ruled them.

An era of great journeys

1488 Bartholomew Diaz (from Portugal) explores the coast of Africa and rounds the Cape of Good Hope to find the Indian Ocean.

1492 Christopher Columbus (from Spain) reaches the West Indies.

1497 John Cabot (from Britain) explores the coasts of Newfoundland.

1500 Pedro Alvares Cabral (from Portugal) lands on the Brazilian coast.

1520 Ferdinand Magellan (from Spain) reaches the Pacific from the South Atlantic.

1535 Jacques Cartier (from France) sails up the St. Lawrence River.

1578 Francis Drake (from Great Britain) discovers Cape Horn.

*Left: An old Portuguese church overlooks a market in the Brazilian city of Recife. The Portuguese settled this coast in the 1530s and brought African slaves to work on their sugar-cane fields. Many Brazilians today are **descendants** of Portuguese and African people.*

Present-Day Settlements

The most densely populated shores of the Atlantic lie along the coasts of the industrial and developed countries of Europe and North America. The deepwater bays and inlets of the northwest Atlantic coast provided safe and large harbors for the first settlers in North America. Large cities such as New York, Boston, Philadelphia, Washington, and Baltimore have grown up here. Around these Atlantic ports spread huge industrial areas where **raw materials** that are brought in by ship can be processed.

On the other side of the Atlantic, European cities such as Liverpool and Bristol in Britain, Bordeaux in France, and Lisbon in Portugal were some of the busiest Atlantic ports. Today, these ports are not as important because there is less shipping trade across the Atlantic. Other ports, such as Rotterdam in The Netherlands, which is closer to the heart of Europe, have taken their shipping business.

Lands around the South Atlantic are far less developed, although this is changing fast. The main built-up areas along the Atlantic coasts of South America lie near Rio de Janeiro and Santos in Brazil, and along the Plate River between Uruguay and Argentina. Large stretches of the West African coastline have few people, partly because deserts (the Sahara and Namib) reach down to the Atlantic and the lack of freshwater makes settlement difficult. However, along the coasts of equatorial West

Movement of People

Settlements in America grew rapidly as people left Europe because of wars, poverty, and overcrowding, hoping to start new lives where land was cheap and plentiful. From 1840–1900 about 20 million people crossed the Atlantic from Europe to the United States. Another huge movement across the Atlantic took place between the sixteenth and the nineteenth centuries, when about 10 million Africans were transported by force from Africa to the Americas to work as slaves for the white settlers. Once captured, Africans were brought to the coast and European traders loaded them onto ships, keeping them in appalling conditions on the long journey across the Atlantic Ocean.

Africa are large, growing cities such as Lagos in Nigeria, Accra in Ghana, and Dakar in Senegal.

Outside the busy cities, Atlantic coasts with their small villages and wild scenery are gradually changing as tourists visit the seaside in larger and larger numbers. Along many of the North Atlantic shores there are holiday homes or resorts, and tourism has become one of the main sources of income for coastal people. In the South Atlantic, there are more places left where villagers live in a traditional way, by fishing for food. Tourism is spreading here too, however, and can bring much-needed money to local people, although it can also change their peaceful way of life forever.

Below: This map shows the larger countries around the Atlantic as well as some of the important ports of each continent that faces the ocean.

Left: A popular beach in the city of Rio de Janeiro, Brazil. Like many of the beautiful Atlantic beaches, tourists flock here to enjoy swimming and sunbathing. Away from the cities, the coasts of Brazil and Africa still have long stretches of sandy beaches that are unspoiled by building.

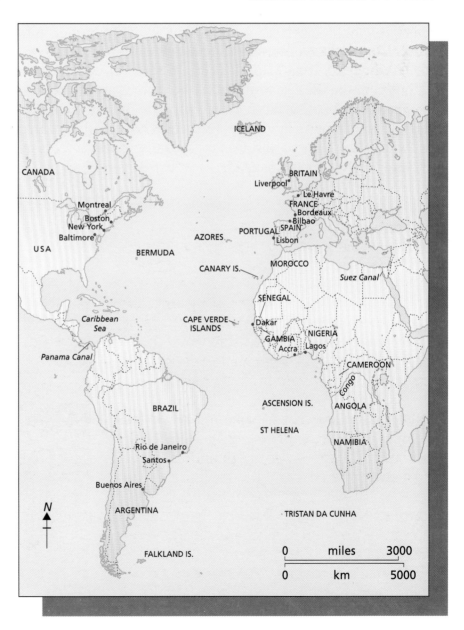

Islands

None of the islands out in the open Atlantic except for the Canary Islands were inhabited before Europeans discovered them. At first, most were used as places to stop off for fresh water and food on the long sailing voyages. Then they were settled by the Portuguese, Spanish, and British, and many of the islanders today are descendants of people from these countries. In St. Helena most people are descendants of East Indian and African slaves who once worked on sugarcane **plantations** belonging to the British.

Many Atlantic islands are very hilly because they are made up of volcanoes, such as Mount Teide, Tenerife, which rises 12,200 feet out of the sea. Some of the volcanoes are still active. The slopes can be difficult to grow **crops** on, but volcanic soil is **fertile** and most islands are farmed. Those with a warm climate like the Azores and Canary Islands produce tropical fruit, like pineapples and bananas, as well as vegetables.

Below: Most of the treeless and windswept land on the remote Falkland Islands is used for sheep farming. Although the islands lie in the far South Atlantic, 310 miles off the coast of Argentina, they are British. Argentina calls them the Islas Malvinas and claims the islands should belong to them.

Islanders also depend on fishing, and in Iceland and the Azores fish are canned and **exported**. For many islanders, the tourist industry has brought a new way of life. People of the Canary Islands, which have a warm climate and are not far from Europe, now make their living from the thousands of European vacationers who visit every year.

Most of the islands in the Atlantic lie far from the mainland. Lonely Ascension Island, in the middle of the Atlantic, is only seven miles across and has bare volcanic mountain ranges. It is used mainly as an airbase because there are only small parts of the island that can be farmed. The nearest land to Bermuda is the east coast of the United States, 600 miles away, and because the island has few natural resources, nearly everything has to be imported. But because it lies on an important ocean route between America and Europe, and has beautiful scenery that encourages tourists, Bermuda has become a wealthy island.

Above: São Miguel, the largest island in the Azores in the middle of the Atlantic. The Azores are peaks of underwater volcanoes that rise up from the Mid-Atlantic Ridge. The islanders farm cattle, and vegetables and fruit grow well in the warm and wet climate.

Changing Trade Patterns

The Atlantic explorers of the fifteenth century were trying to find new sea routes to the Far East to trade in spices and silks, which were greatly valued by Europeans. Their discovery of the Americas opened a new and very important area of trade. At first most of the crossings were made by adventurers and explorers, searching for riches; some made fortunes shipping gold back from South America to Europe. During the seventeenth and eighteenth centuries, when people settled along the coasts of the Americas, ships began regular crossings from Europe to bring supplies and to take back what the colonies had to sell.

As the settlements in the Americas grew, so did trade across the Atlantic. Between 1840 and 1900, the population of the United States increased from 17 million to nearly 76 million and the amount of trade increased 10 times. Until the end of World War II, the North Atlantic was the busiest shipping route in the world.

Below: A container ship sails along the Suez Canal. The canal was cut through the Egyptian desert in 1869 to link the Mediterranean Sea to the Indian Ocean. It changed trading routes in the Atlantic because ships could avoid traveling thousands of miles through the South Atlantic and around southern Africa.

Above: The busy waterfront at the port of Manaus on the Amazon River, nearly 1,200 miles from the Atlantic Ocean. The huge river is a waterway that even oceangoing ships can use to travel far inland from the sea. In the late 1800s, rubber was shipped from here down the Amazon and across the Atlantic to the United States and Europe.

Although many ships still cross the Atlantic today, the great flow of traffic to and from Europe is less than it once was. Colonies that were once tied to the European country that ruled them are now independent and free to trade anywhere. There are also new markets in other parts of the world—for example, a lot of cargo is now traveling from North America across the Pacific Ocean because trade with Asian countries is growing.

Shipping routes also changed when the Suez and Panama canals were built. The Suez Canal in Egypt, which was opened in 1869, linked the Mediterranean Sea with the Indian Ocean, and ships from Europe no longer need to travel many thousands of miles through the South Atlantic to reach the Far East. Using the Panama Canal in Central America, ships can also avoid long journeys through the South Atlantic to reach the Pacific Ocean.

TRADE AND TRANSPORTATION
Atlantic Cargoes

The early colonies in the Americas produced luxury goods that fetched high prices in Europe and made it worth the long and expensive trip across the ocean. From Canada came furs, from America tobacco, and from the West Indies and Brazil the main product was sugarcane. The colonies needed people to work on the plantations, so slaves were brought across the Atlantic from Africa. Gradually, a triangle of trade developed, from Europe to West Africa to buy slaves, then to the Americas where slaves were sold, and then back across the Atlantic to Europe with goods from the colonies.

The shipping of slaves across the Atlantic finally ended in 1865, but by then passenger ships were carrying thousands of people, the new settlers, across the ocean. Farm produce continued to be sent back to Europe, but during the late 1800s, industries grew rapidly in North America. Raw materials and manufactured goods gradually became more important cargoes.

Modern Atlantic trade consists mostly of transporting bulky raw materials such as coal, iron ore, oil, and other minerals from places where they are extracted (for example, oil from the Middle East, Nigeria, and Venezuela) to the industrial

Left: Bananas grow best in the warm climate of tropical countries. From places such as Africa and South America, they are loaded onto boats and shipped to countries around the North Atlantic.

Above: A container ship at Le Havre, a big Atlantic port in France. The containers are brought to the port on trucks or by trains and are easily loaded on and off the ship by cranes.

centers of Europe and North America. Here the raw materials are used to make goods, and then the finished products, such as machinery, are exported again by sea. Chemicals and cars are some of the main goods that leave the shores of North America.

The United States and Canada also have natural resources such as coal and timber, which are exported across the Atlantic. Wheat grown in the heart of North America is sent by ship down the St. Lawrence Seaway, across the Atlantic to Russia, Africa, and the Middle East. South America still exports farm produce such as meat, cereals, and fruit to the industrial countries around the North Atlantic, but ships also bring cars, textiles, and chemicals from new industrial centers.

Crossing the Atlantic

The Vikings used their knowledge of winds and currents to make long, dangerous journeys in simple sail boats; now computer-controlled ships cross from North America to Europe in just a few days. During the years of great exploration, Europeans learned a lot about **navigating** the ocean. But the type and speed of ships changed dramatically

Below: On the northeast coast of Brazil, fishermen use these small sailing boats, called jangadas, to catch fish. Jangadas are used only for sailing close to the coast, not for sailing far out into the ocean.

Right: The QE2 was built in 1967 to carry passengers across the Atlantic between the United States and Europe. Few people now cross the Atlantic by ship because the journey is so much quicker by airplane.

in the 1800s, when trade across the North Atlantic was at its busiest. Shipbuilders were racing to build the fastest ship. Until the mid-1800s, the United States built the best sailing ships, such as the very fast, streamlined **clippers**, but then the British started building steamships, which did not have to rely on winds. By 1900, the large sailing ship was a thing of the past.

Shipbuilding was big business in many ports, like New York, and Liverpool in Great Britain. As well as cargo ships, the great dockyards built passenger liners like the *Lusitania* and *Mauretania*, which were launched in 1906. One of the last Atlantic passenger liners to be built was the British *Queen Elizabeth 2 (QE2)*, in 1967; it is now used only as a luxury cruise ship by tourists.

Although the first airplane crossed the Atlantic as early as 1919, it was some time before regular flights were made. By the 1950s, it was becoming cheaper and quicker for people to travel by air. When airplanes with jet engines started to be used in the 1960s, passenger ships were no longer used for crossing the Atlantic.

Ships are still used in the Atlantic because they are the cheapest way to transport bulky and heavy goods across the sea. About one-third of all ships crossing the Atlantic are bulk oil-carriers, mostly huge **supertankers**. The other important kind of ship is the container ship, where goods are put into large, boxlike containers, which makes them easy to load and unload onto ships from trucks or trains.

Ports

Although there are natural deepwater bays where ships can safely moor and unload, much of the Atlantic coastline has dangerous shallows and shifting sands. Most Atlantic ports lie in river estuaries where the water is deeper and there is shelter from the open ocean. Rivers are often the easiest route to take goods inland. On rivers such as the Amazon, Brazil, the St. Lawrence, Canada, the Seine, France, and the Niger, Nigeria, goods are unloaded at ports that are large enough for oceangoing ships. The goods are then transferred to smaller boats and barges to be taken upriver.

New York

When Henry Hudson explored the mouth of the Hudson River in 1609, he described it as a magnificent harbor, sheltered by green hills with good farming land all around. The city of New York now lies there, the largest and busiest Atlantic port of all. The center of the city is on Manhattan Island, where many miles of docks were built on the long waterfronts that are surrounded by deep water channels. New docks have now been built on the mainland to handle giant supertankers and container ships. Oil refineries, flour mills, chemical works, and other factories spread in all directions around the port, to process the goods brought in by ships.

However, river estuaries have problems. Rivers bring down a huge amount of mud and other material and drop it near their mouths, which often makes the water very shallow. Like many others, the mouth of the Seine River near the busy Atlantic port of Le Havre has to be constantly **dredged** and deepened to allow large ships through.

Left: Port Jerome oil refinery on the Seine River in France

Above: New York City, at the mouth of the Hudson River. New York is the largest port on the Atlantic. Once there were docks all around the island, but new and larger docks have been built on the mainland nearby.

The offshore line of sandbars and beaches along the U.S. coastline also makes it difficult and dangerous for ships—part of this coast is nicknamed the Graveyard of the Atlantic because so many ships have sunk here. To make a safer route along this coast, a series of artificial canals now link bays, lagoons, and rivers to make a long waterway parallel to the coast, stretching from Boston to Florida. This is called the Atlantic Intracoastal Waterway.

Atlantic ports are not just places for ships to moor. They have huge cranes to handle goods quickly, and warehouses or tanks to store every kind of material. The most successful Atlantic ports also have good roads and railroads so that goods can be transported easily inland. Nearly all Atlantic ports have had to be rebuilt at some time, or new ports constructed nearby, because modern ships are so huge. Bordeaux, France, for example, has five new outports to handle large tankers and container ships.

Fishing

Fish are a very important source of food for the many millions of people living around the Atlantic, but nowhere is as heavily fished as the North Atlantic. The developed countries of Europe and North America, with their huge populations and fishing fleets, have trawled the rich fishing grounds for years in the cold northern waters. The main fishing areas of the North Atlantic are the Grand Banks off Newfoundland and the seas around Iceland and Great Britain.

Farming the Atlantic

In coastal waters off Canada, Scotland, and Norway, salmon and sea trout are reared in special cages or tanks that float in the open sea. The fish have to be regularly fed because they cannot swim freely to find their own food. In shallow waters off the coasts of France and Spain, shellfish such as oysters and mussels are kept in enclosures that fill with seawater. North American fish farmers raise clams, mussels, and oysters. Fish farming is a way of providing seafood without having to go fishing, but it is not easy raising fish like this.

Among the most important fish caught in the North Atlantic are cod and haddock, and in the South Atlantic, hake. Crustaceans (lobsters, crabs, and prawns) are caught off the coast of North America and in warmer waters of the Atlantic, such as off the coast of Brazil. The cold waters along the West African coast are rich in sardines and anchovies. Although African countries have their own fishing fleets, many other nations also come to fish off the coast.

Below: A fisherman hauls in his net on the coast of Gambia. On many Atlantic coasts, people still use simple nets like these to catch small amounts of fish, which are their main source of food.

Along some Atlantic coasts, especially in the South Atlantic, people still fish for their own food. Their catch is usually small, and they seldom travel far from the coast. However, 90 percent of the fish caught in the sea are taken by commercial fishing boats to sell what they catch. Using nets many miles long, modern fishing trawlers can scoop up huge schools of fish in one haul.

Left: Most people of the Faeroe Islands in the North Atlantic depend on fishing for their livelihood. This fisherman is unloading halibut, a large flat-fish. Overfishing has meant that halibut is becoming more difficult to find and catch.

Before fishing boats started refrigerating fish in the 1960s, fish were preserved using salt and later ice to keep them fresh. Now, by freezing fish, trawlers can stay at sea for as long as six months until their holds are full. Commercial fishing boats travel long distances away from their home ports, and even Japanese trawlers can be seen fishing off the coasts of West Africa.

Below: The layout of a typical freezer trawler. Below decks is a large cold store where fish can be frozen and stored while the boat is still at sea. A boat like this can catch many tons of fish before it needs to return to port. Three-quarters of commercially caught fish is eaten by humans, and the rest is made into animal food.

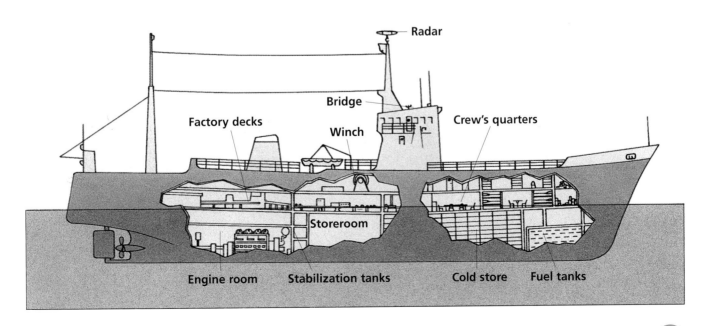

Radar

Bridge

Factory decks

Winch

Crew's quarters

Storeroom

Engine room

Stabilization tanks

Cold store

Fuel tanks

Mineral Resources

Getting minerals from the earth on land is easier than getting them from the sea. But as resources from the land become used up and harder to find, people have turned to the sea. Exploring for minerals and extracting them is very difficult in the Atlantic because the ocean is so deep, so most mining is done on the continental shelves, where waters are shallower and it is easier to reach the seabed.

Oil is drilled off the West African coast in Nigeria and in smaller amounts in Cameroon, the Congo, and Angola. In the 1980s, Nigeria was one of the top 10 oil-producing countries in the world.

It is not always necessary to drill into the seabed to get minerals. Placer deposits are minerals washed out of rocks that settle on the seabed close to shore. Off Namibia in southwest Africa, placer deposits of diamonds lie along the coast, and these are collected by dredging the shore. The diamonds are then sorted from the sand.

One of the biggest mineral-extraction industries around the Atlantic is for sand and gravel, used in constructing buildings and roads. Where currents close to the coast sweep sand and pebbles into heaps, these are often dredged from the sea. One of the largest offshore mining operations in the Atlantic is on Great Bahamas Bank, where there are especially fine sands, used in making cement and glass.

Although it is believed there are many more valuable minerals in the rocks under the sea, Atlantic resources are still mostly unexplored. The Mid-Atlantic Ridge is

Below: Manganese nodules were first discovered on the deep ocean floor. They are hard lumps of rock, full of valuable metals. No one has yet found an easy way of getting them off the seabed because they lie so far beneath the surface of the sea.

Above: Salt is the most common mineral in seawater. Here in Namibia, seawater is fed into shallow ponds and the water evaporates in the sun, leaving the salt behind. It is scooped up and put into piles ready to be loaded into trucks to be sold.

one area that is being surveyed in the hope of finding minerals in enough quantities to make deep-sea mining worth it. Elsewhere, manganese nodules (lumps of rock that are rich in minerals) have been found scattered along the deep-ocean floor. Unfortunately, they lie 13,000 feet underwater and no one has yet found a way of collecting them that is not too expensive.

RESOURCES OF THE ATLANTIC
Sea Power

The sea is constantly moving with tides and waves. This natural energy can be used to make power. One of the first power generators ever to use tidal energy lies on the Rance River, on the French coast. A 2,625 foot-long barrier was built across the river near its mouth. As the tide comes in and goes out, the water now passes through tunnels in the barrier. Inside each tunnel is a generator, which is turned by the water and makes electricity. Another tidal power station has been built in the Bay of Fundy in Canada.

The Atlantic Ocean has many bays and river estuaries where there is a great difference between high- and low-tide levels, but so far there are few tidal power generators because they are very expensive to build, and other ways of making electricity, such as burning coal, are still cheaper.

Below: Here, near the mouth of the Rance River in France a dam-like barrier makes use of the power of tidal water. As tides come in and out, water is forced through tunnels in the barrier. The water turns a generator that makes electricity.

As natural resources like oil and coal run out, tidal power from the Atlantic may become more common—and it has the advantage of not causing **pollution** in the air or water.

Wave energy could be an even more valuable source of free power, especially along windswept North Atlantic coasts where waves constantly pound the shore. However, no one has yet found an efficient way of getting enough power from wave energy, although experiments have been tried using rafts that bob up and down with the waves and turn generators. The main problem with waves is that they cannot be relied on because they vary in size and direction so much, depending on the weather. This means that they cannot always produce enough power to be used on a large scale.

Above: Waves pound the rocky shores in the Canary Islands. If the energy of the restless waves could be captured, it could be used to make power. People have come up with several ideas, but the problem of how to get the electricity generated from the sea to the land where it is needed has yet to be solved.

CHANGING OCEAN
Overfishing

Fish numbers are falling all over the Atlantic due to overfishing, and many **species** of fish have been affected. Since the 1950s, such huge amounts of cod have been caught off the coast of Newfoundland in Canada that by the late 1980s, numbers had seriously declined. In 1992 the Canadians stopped cod fishing altogether, fearing that the fish would disappear. When one kind of fish becomes difficult to find, fishermen roam the seas to find another—in the North Atlantic, trawlers now hunt the less-valuable turbot instead of cod.

No one is exactly sure what the effects of overfishing will be, but if it carries on, the fish will not be able to breed quickly enough to survive. All the creatures and plants of the Atlantic depend on one another for food. If one species disappears, this could upset the balance in the natural food chain.

In the last 20 years, the number of fishing boats on ocean waters has doubled, and modern equipment allows fishermen to catch more fish than ever before. The huge nets sweep up everything in the ocean, some scraping the ocean floor and killing all kinds of life. Fish that are not wanted by the fishermen are thrown back dead into the water.

Many people around the world depend on fish for their survival. When Canada closed its cod industry, based in Newfoundland, 40,000 jobs were lost; the people had few other ways of making a living. There are other Atlantic nations such as Iceland and Spain with many people in the fishing industry who would have a hard time if they were unable to catch fish.

Whaling

There are many species of whales in the Atlantic. During the last hundred years, vast numbers have been killed by commercial fishermen. There used to be whaling stations on the northeast coast of the United States and on South Georgia in the South Atlantic, where the whales were taken to be processed for meat and oil. One species of whale after another was hunted until, during the 1980s, an international ban was placed on commercial whaling. However, the Northern Right whale that feeds in the Gulf of Maine is in danger of disappearing altogether.

Right: The rusting remains of a whaling ship and whaling station on the island of South Georgia in the South Atlantic

In poorer nations, overfishing can leave people even worse off. For example, Senegal allows many trawlers from the **European Union** to fish in its waters. In one catch, a single foreign trawler can scoop up to 2,000 tons of fish, about the same as 1,500 traditional boats might collect. Local fishermen find their own catches getting smaller and their food disappearing.

Right: *As more fishing boats go out to sea, the numbers of some species of fish are falling to seriously low levels, especially in the North Atlantic. If fishing is controlled and managed properly, the ocean could easily provide us with plenty of food.*

Polluted Waters

Billions of tons of garbage are thrown into the Atlantic every year. Human **sewage**, household garbage, chemical waste from factories, and chemicals sprayed on farmland all find their way into rivers or pour directly out into the sea. Although these are the main sources of sea pollution, some comes from ships at sea. Oil spilled from wrecked oil tankers, like the *Amoco Cadiz* that sank off the rough Atlantic coast of France in 1978, had serious effects on wildlife, and can kill shore creatures and birds. Ships carrying oil and chemicals also use seawater to wash out their tanks.

Although the open seas of the Atlantic are still relatively clean, coastal areas are heavily polluted, especially those close to cities. The effects are worse in bays and river estuaries, such as Chesapeake Bay, which receives the waste from 8 million people and chemicals from thousands of factories.

Below: Even on the remote Falkland Islands, beaches are polluted with plastic and other garbage thrown overboard from ships and washed up on the shore. Sea creatures and birds are sometimes killed when they become entangled in the garbage.

Above: The Amoco Cadiz *oil tanker ran aground off the coast of France in 1978. Oil spilled out into the sea and washed up on beaches, polluting the shoreline and killing all kinds of wildlife. This disaster hit the headlines, but most pollution around Atlantic shores comes from the chemicals, garbage, and sewage that we dump into the ocean every day.*

Garbage, oil, and human sewage make beaches unpleasant and sometimes dangerous and unusable. In 1988, beaches around New York City had to be closed because of dangerous waste being washed ashore. Pollution can also make people ill, and poisonous chemicals can stay in fish and shellfish a long time without causing them any obvious harm. In Canada, people have died from eating mussels found later to be full of dangerous levels of poisons.

Creatures and plants in the sea can actually help break down certain waste, like human sewage, but not the vast amounts that are pumped into the sea from large cities. Chemicals cause more serious problems. These either kill life in the sea or cause damage and diseases. Cancers found in beluga whales in the St. Lawrence River estuary in Canada are thought to be due to chemicals from an aluminum factory. In all heavily polluted coastal areas and estuaries, the variety of sea life is much less than it once was.

43

CHANGING OCEAN
Managing the Atlantic

Many people see the Atlantic as a free and endless source of food and a convenient place to dump garbage. This viewpoint did not matter when the population around the ocean was small, but now that overfishing and pollution are serious threats, the ocean needs to be used carefully.

There are some restrictions on fishing. Each country has an Exclusive Economic Zone (EEZ), an area up to 200 miles off its coastline, which it controls. Many countries set quotas, which are limits on how many fish can be caught and how many days their fishermen can go out to sea. The European Union has laws on the size of fishing net holes, so younger and smaller fish do not get caught and can have a chance to breed. Beyond the EEZs, the Atlantic is open to anyone. Some international agreements ban the hunting of certain species of fish that are in the greatest danger, but it is very difficult to get countries to agree and impossible to make sure they do not break the rules.

Below: The ship Solo *belongs to Greenpeace, an environmental group that tries to explain to people about the damage we can do to our oceans, especially by overfishing and pollution.*

Above: In the Faeroe Islands in the North Atlantic, pilot whales are driven ashore in a yearly hunt. Although most whaling is banned, some small communities are allowed to continue their traditional killing of whales.

The richer countries of the North Atlantic have pollution controls over the treatment of human sewage and chemicals that factories pour out into the rivers and sea. Even so, the laws are not strict enough and are not always followed. Huge amounts of waste produced by these industrialized countries still pollute the Atlantic.

Developing countries, such as those in Africa and South America, which are struggling to catch up with richer nations, cannot afford to spend money on controlling pollution of the seas around them.

No one is sure of the long-term effects of some of the chemical pollution on life in the Atlantic because so much of this vast ocean is still unknown. If the living resources of the Atlantic are to last into the future, people need to learn more about how the ocean works, as well as controlling how it is used.

Glossary

civilizations Communities with a high level of art, customs, and laws.

clippers Very fast sailing ships with large sails.

colony A country that has been settled or conquered by another country and which is then ruled or governed by that country.

container ship A ship that carries goods in large metal boxes. The boxes are of a standard size so they can easily be transferred on to ships, trains, and trucks when they arrive on land.

continental shelf A gently sloping area of sea floor that continues out from a continent under the sea.

continents Large areas of land, such as North America or Africa.

crops Plants that are grown for food.

deltas Flat, fan-shaped areas that form where rivers split into many channels as they reach the sea.

descendants Relatives of people who lived long ago.

dredge To dig out mud, gravel, or sand from the bottom of rivers, harbors, or the sea.

equator An imaginary line that circles the middle of the Earth.

estuaries The mouths of rivers where they open out as they near the sea. Fresh-water mixes with saltwater here. The effects of tides can be felt in estuaries.

European Union An organization of twelve European countries that work together.

exports Goods sold to foreign countries.

fertile Rich in nutrients that help plants grow well.

generators Machines that make electricity.

hurricanes Violent tropical storms.

lagoons Areas of saltwater, separated from the sea by sandbanks.

latitudes Distances north and south of the equator.

legends Stories from long ago.

mammals Animals that are warm-blooded. Mammals give birth to live young that they feed with their own milk.

migrations Regular journeys made by some species of animal, usually at certain times of year, in search of food or a special place to breed.

natural resources Natural products people can use.

navigating Finding the best route across water (or land).

plantations Places where crops are grown on a large scale and then sold for money.

pollution The introduction of any material or energy into the environment that has a damaging effect.

raw materials Basic substances, such as minerals, from which other goods are made.

sewage Waste from houses and factories.

silt Very fine mud or clay that is carried by a river.

slaves People who are forced to work for others, against their will and without being paid.

spawn To lay eggs in water.

species Groups of animals or plants that are similar.

supertankers Very large ships designed to carry liquid cargo.

tidal ranges The differences in height between successive high and low waters.

trading posts Stores, usually in remote places, where goods are brought to sell.

tropical The climate of the regions lying either side of the equator.

volcanic Used to describe something caused by the eruption of a volcano.

Further Information

There are very few books about the Atlantic Ocean itself, so look for general books about seas and oceans, the countries that lie along the shores of the Atlantic, and the rivers that flow out into the ocean. These are some books that might be useful:

FOR YOUNGER READERS:

Baines, John, *Protecting the Oceans* (Conserving Our World Series). Austin, TX: Raintree Steck-Vaughn, 1990.

Collins, Elizabeth. *The Living Ocean* (Earth at Risk Series). New York: Chelsea House, 1994.

Eyewitness Staff. *Ocean*. New York: Random House, 1995.

Lambert, David and McConnell, Anita. *Seas and Oceans* (World of Science Series). New York: Facts on File, 1985.

FOR OLDER READERS:

Middleton, Nick. *Atlas of the Natural World*. World Contemporary Issues. New York: Facts on File, 1991.

Stevenson, R. E., and Talbot, F. H., editors. *Oceans*. New York: Time-Life, 1993.

CD ROMS:

Geopedia: The Multimedia Geography CD-Rom. Chicago: Encyclopedia Britannica.

USEFUL ADDRESSES:

Center for Environmental Education, Center for Marine Conservation, 1725 De Sales Street NW, Suite 500, Washington, DC 20036

Earthwatch Headquarters, 680 Mount Auburn Street, P.O. Box 403, Watertown, MA 02272-9104

Index